D0287774

by MARC TYLER NOBLEMAN
illustrated by BRADFORD KENDALL

STONE ARCH BOOKS
www.stonearchbooks.com

Shade Books are published by Stone Arch Books
151 Good Counsel Drive, P.O. Box 669
Mankato, Minnesota 56002
www.stonearchbooks.com

Library of Congress Cataloging-in-Publication Data
Nobleman, Marc Tyler.
Little lightning / by Marc Tyler Nobleman ; illustrated by Bradford Kendall.
p. cm.
"Shade Books"—T.p. verso.
Summary: Fourteen-year-old Mary has always been drawn to the woods near her friend Isobel's home, but Isobel does not understand why until the aftereffects of a lightning storm force Mary to reveal a long-kept secret.
ISBN 978-1-4342-1613-7 (lib. bdg.)
[1. Supernatural—Fiction. 2. Forests and forestry—Fiction. 3. Gnomes—Fiction. 4. Fathers and daughters—Fiction. 5. Environmental protection—Fiction.] I. Kendall, Bradford, ill. II. Title.
PZ7.N67154Lit 2010
[Fic]—dc22

2009003781

Creative Director: Heather Kindseth
Graphic Designer: Hilary Wacholz

1 2 3 4 5 6 13 12 11 10 09 08

Printed in the United States of America

TABLE OF CONTENTS

Chapter 1

THE STORM

Mary and Isabel ran out of the woods into a field. Even though it was not yet five o'clock on a June afternoon, it didn't look much lighter out in the open than it had underneath the trees. The sky was full of dark gray clouds.

As Mary ran, she glanced back at the woods.

"Hurry up!" Isabel said, laughing as she ran.

The two 14-year-olds passed several construction vehicles. The trucks had been clearing a part of the forest, but now they were parked and empty.

Mary and Isabel kept running. They crossed the grassy field, then ran down a gravel road.

Finally, they ended up on Isabel's family's farm. As they headed toward the barn, it began to rain.

"Great timing," Isabel said as the girls ran inside the barn.

Mary saw the first flash of lightning through the huge open door. Isabel walked over to Red Delicious, her horse, who was the only animal in the barn.

She patted him on his nose. Then she plopped down on a bale of hay.

“You and that forest,” Isabel said, turning to look at Mary. “It’s harder to get you to leave there than it is to get Brianna Harrison to leave the mall. You know that girl loves her shopping.”

The girls laughed. Then Isabel looked serious.

“We’ve been doing these forest field trips since third grade,” Isabel said. “I just don’t think there’s anything left to discover.”

She looked carefully at Mary’s face. Then Isabel went on, “Don’t get me wrong. It’s really pretty in there, and the butterflies are cool, but we’re not little girls anymore. I mean, look what other girls our age are into. Besides Brianna, of course. Other girls aren’t just hanging out in the forest all the time.”

"It's not like I force you to come with me," Mary said, frowning. "It's okay if you don't want to go."

"But you never want to do anything else," Isabel said.

"We went to that basketball game together, like you wanted to," Mary pointed out. "That was something else. That didn't involve the forest."

"That was baseball, and it was five months ago," Isabel said as lightning flickered. "I know you feel, like, grateful or something to the forest, but whatever it was that happened to you there happened a long time ago."

Thunder shook the barn. Mary stood up and walked to the door. She was taking slow, deep breaths.

"I'm sorry," Isabel said. "I'm such a jerk. I didn't mean to hurt you. But as your best friend, I do think it's time for you to move on."

Mary took one more deep breath. "Okay," she said. "Let's move on. Or at least go in. I'm sure your mom has dinner waiting for us."

* * *

After dinner, the storm got worse, so Mary decided to stay over. After Isabel brushed her teeth, she walked back into her bedroom.

Mary was standing by the window, staring at the forest.

Isabel walked over. "I hope you're not still upset," she said.

Just then, bolts of lightning stabbed into the forest. Mary and Isabel stared as flames burst up into the stormy sky.

Chapter 2

TO THE FOREST

"That lightning hit the forest!" Mary said. "That was incredible."

"I've never seen a fire start in a rainstorm before," Isabel said. "That's some serious heat."

Mary leaned toward the window and squinted. It looked like the rain put out the fire right away. She turned and walked toward the door. "Are you done in the bathroom?" she asked.

"Yeah," Isabel said. She continued to look out the window.

After a few minutes, when Mary didn't come back, Isabel went into the hallway. The bathroom door was closed and the light was on, but no sound came from inside.

"Mary?" Isabel said.

She knocked, but there was no answer. She tried the door and it opened. Mary was not there.

Isabel hurried down the stairs, trying to be quiet so that she wouldn't wake her parents. At the front door, she looked at the mat where she and Mary had left their muddy shoes earlier that evening.

Mary's shoes were gone.

Mary, are you nuts? she thought.

As another streak of lightning flooded the dark house, Isabel took a flashlight from the coat closet. She also grabbed an umbrella. Then she quietly stepped outside.

Thunder rumbled in the sky. The rain came down straight and steady. Shining the flashlight over the ground before her, Isabel saw fresh footprints in the mud.

She glanced nervously at the house over her shoulder. Her parents' window was dark. She began to walk through the field, following the tracks Mary had left.

Soon, she saw a hooded figure a few yards ahead.

"Don't tell me you're going to the forest!" Isabel called.

"It's okay," Mary yelled back. "Don't worry."

Isabel ran up to Mary and said, "Come on. Let's get back inside before my parents wake up."

"You go," Mary said. "I'll be fine. I'll be back soon. Trust me."

"Come on," Isabel said. "You're being ridiculous. Let's go back. We're going to get struck by lightning standing here."

Mary shook her head. "I have to go," she said. She started to walk toward the forest.

"I'm not leaving you out here," Isabel said, reaching out to grab her friend.

A screechy hiss erupted behind them. The whole area suddenly glowed red. The girls turned to see more flames. This time, they were coming from the direction of Isabel's farm.

Chapter 3

UNUSUAL LIGHTNING

"No!" Isabel screamed.

She tossed the flashlight to Mary and began to run back toward the farm. Mary followed her.

As they neared the farm, they saw that the barn was on fire. The rain had lightened, and it wasn't putting out the fire. The lights were on in the house.

"Red Delicious!" Isabel called. She sprinted into the barn.

"Isabel!" Mary shouted. She dropped the flashlight and followed Isabel. Something brushed against her ankle. She looked down, but saw nothing.

As the walls burned around her, Isabel struggled to open her horse's gate. Red Delicious was snorting and bucking. His eyes were wide with fear.

Isabel's hands shook and she began to scream. Mary took a deep breath. Calmly, she opened the gate.

Both girls guided Red Delicious out of the barn. As she left, Mary thought she saw something weird on the ground near the door. She didn't stop to see what it was.

The girls ran to the front door of Isabel's house. Isabel hugged her horse's neck tightly.

Red Delicious was still panicked, but he seemed to know he was out of danger. Isabel looped the horse's reins around a porch post.

Isabel heard fire engine sirens coming closer. Her parents rushed out of the house and pulled Isabel and Mary close to them. Though the girls' clothes were burned, neither of them was hurt. Isabel's dad held a large umbrella over them all.

"I'm so glad you two are okay," Isabel's mom said.

The group stood, shocked, as they watched the barn burn.

The first fire engine pulled up. A firefighter jumped off, rushed to the house, and pointed at the barn. It was Kyle, one of Isabel's neighbors.

"Anyone in there? Any animals?" Kyle yelled.

Isabel and Mary shook their heads. "We got the horse out," Isabel told him.

"You all okay?" Kyle asked. They nodded. He ran back to his team.

In only a minute, the fire was out. The barn smoked as the rain continued to fall. What was left of the building looked like a giant, black spider.

Kyle walked back over. "Sorry about your barn," he said.

"Thank you, Kyle," Isabel's mom said.

"Do you know what caused it?" Isabel's father asked.

Kyle shook his head. "We're looking into that right now," he said.

He looked at Isabel and Mary and asked, "Do you girls know anything about this?"

"Why were you two outside?" Mom added.

"We were just checking on Red Delicious," Isabel said, patting the horse on his nose. Mary looked down. "You know how scared he gets when it thunders," Isabel added.

"We were heading back inside," Mary said. "Then lightning struck the barn."

"Thanks," Kyle said. "I'll let you all know what we find out."

The firefighters looked through the charred, soggy remains of the barn for about ten minutes. Then Kyle walked back over to the group.

"Strange," he said. "We found where we think the fire started. It looks like lightning hit the barn, just like Mary said."

"What's strange about that?" Isabel's dad asked. "There was a lot of lightning tonight."

"Yes, but lightning usually strikes the top of something," Kyle said. "Follow me. I want to show you something."

Isabel, Mary, and Isabel's parents walked over to the smoking remains of the barn. Kyle shined his flashlight on an area that looked like it had been blasted with intense heat. It was at the very bottom of an outside wall.

"See?" Kyle asked. "Right at the bottom of the barn. Not where lightning would normally strike. Your fire started there."

Chapter 4

WHOSE HAT?

The group examined the spot on the barn that Kyle's flashlight had pointed to.

"How could lightning do that?" Mary asked. She looked nervously at the woods.

"Beats me," Kyle said. "But if a match or candle had started this, you wouldn't have a darkened blast site like that. It just doesn't make sense either way."

"That's really strange," Isabel said. "I can't imagine what happened."

"The important thing now is that you're all okay," Kyle said. "I'll come by tomorrow and help you clean up." He joined the other firefighters. Soon, the trucks left.

Isabel's dad said, "I should make some calls. I'll find a place for Red Delicious to stay until we can build a new barn." He and Isabel's mother headed inside.

"I want to get another look at that burn mark," Mary told Isabel.

"If you're lying, you know I'll chase you down again," Isabel said. She walked over to her horse.

With the flashlight, Mary walked toward the barn, looking carefully at the ground. The flashlight shined on something small and red. Mary bent over and carefully picked it up.

It was shaped like a tiny red ice-cream cone and was about two inches tall. The piece of fabric looked like a doll's hat. When she saw Isabel coming toward her, Mary quickly slipped the red cone into her pocket.

Isabel looked sadly at the barn. "If you hadn't come outside tonight, we never would've made it to Red Delicious in time," she said. "So thanks for being nuts. But what were you doing?"

"I just wanted to make sure everything was all right," Mary said quietly. "Sorry, I know it's hard for you to understand."

* * *

The next morning, the sky was clear. Mary left before breakfast. But she didn't go home.

Instead, she marched back to the forest. After an hour of walking, Mary saw dozens of tiny blue butterflies flitting through the trees. Then she began to feel a strange heat in the air. She kept walking.

Soon, she came to an area where the heat felt even stronger. There were fewer trees. She saw a circular patch of grass.

Mary stepped into the middle of the grass. She took the red cone out of her pocket. She breathed in and out once. Then she asked, "Whose hat is this?"

The leaves around the edge of the grass circle began to move. Mary saw flashes of red, and some green, brown, and white, too, moving between the leaves.

She was surrounded by four-inch-tall gnomes.

Chapter 5

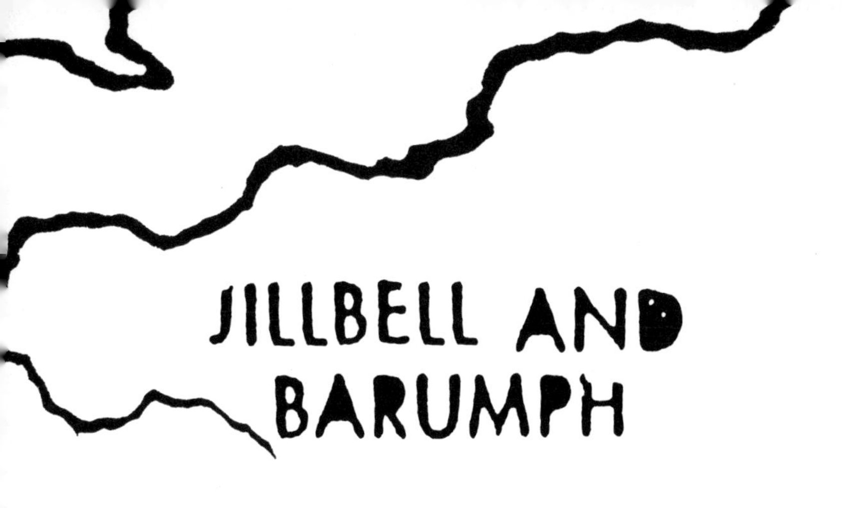

JILLBELL AND BARUMPH

Two gnomes scampered into the grass circle and stopped at Mary's feet. She bent down.

"Mary!" one of the gnomes, a younger girl, said. "It is so nice to see you in our forest. I have not greeted you in so long. Well, I've seen you in the forest, but you are always with your friend."

"Hello, Jillbell," Mary said. "Do you know whose hat this is?"

"It does not matter," said the other gnome, an older male. "Thank you for returning it."

"You're welcome, Barumph," Mary said. "But it does matter. I found the hat near my best friend's barn, right after it burned up. So it matters to me."

Jillbell glanced at Barumph with a disappointed look.

Barumph stood up straight. "The barn was empty," he said.

"A horse was in there!" Mary said. "I thought you were protectors of animals!"

"We protect forest animals," Barumph said. "But last night, we had to act quickly. Unfortunately, that meant not taking care of the humans' horse."

"You lit the barn on fire, Papa?" Jillbell asked sadly.

"You almost killed people!" Mary said.

"Careful, Mary. You may be bigger than me, but I'm still your elder. Do not speak to me like that," Barumph said.

Mary shook her head. "You committed a major crime. You can't scold me for getting angry about it!"

"We do not live by your laws," Barumph said. "And your kind clearly does not care about ours."

"Papa, Mary is our friend," Jillbell said.

"My kind ignores your laws because they don't know about you," Mary said. "I told you I'd keep you a secret, and I have kept my promise."

"You also said you'd keep machines out of the forest," Barumph said. "In the last moon cycle alone, they have killed five more gnomes."

"I've tried to talk my dad out of clearing the forest," Mary told the gnome, "but it's just business to him. It's not like he'll change his job because his daughter annoys him about the environment."

"Please, Papa," Jillbell said. "Don't do anything more." The little gnome paused. Then she added, quietly, "Maybe it's time to tell the humans about us."

Barumph glared at his daughter. "I do not want to hear you say that ever again," he said angrily.

"See?" Mary said. "Fathers don't listen to daughters."

Then she asked, "Why is it so hot here?"

Mary looked around. Nearby, she saw several places where lightning had struck the ground.

"Last night, I saw a bunch of lightning come down at once. Did it hit here?" Mary asked quietly.

"Yes," Barumph said. "Three of us died because of it."

"I'm sorry," Mary said. "So sorry." Some gnomes standing nearby began to cry. "I had a feeling," Mary went on. "I wanted to come right away, to see if you were all right."

"You were going to come all the way here to find us? In a thunderstorm?" Jillbell asked.

"I was going to try, though I don't have the underground tunnels and squirrel mounts like you do," Mary said.

She wiped her forehead. "And I still don't get why it's so hot," she added. "The heat from lightning doesn't stick around for this long, usually."

A younger male gnome, one Mary didn't recognize, stepped forward. He put his hand on Barumph's shoulder.

"Your kind have given us a gift," the younger gnome said. "There is a wire buried here, in the ground. We know that if we removed it, your kind would come to replace it and bother us even more. So we let it stay, and we use it, too. It is ugly, but it is also a good place to hang our hunting tools."

"Last night, during the storm, we were stuck underground," Barumph said. "We knew that no animals would be aboveground for us to hunt, so we used the time to check our tools. Sleb and I and several others were hanging our tools on the wire when lightning struck."

"The wire sent electricity into us," Sleb, the younger gnome, said. "Now we can do this."

A group of gnomes stepped forward. They raised their hands and aimed them at a rotting stump. At once, they each released a bolt of blue electricity that rocketed into the stump.

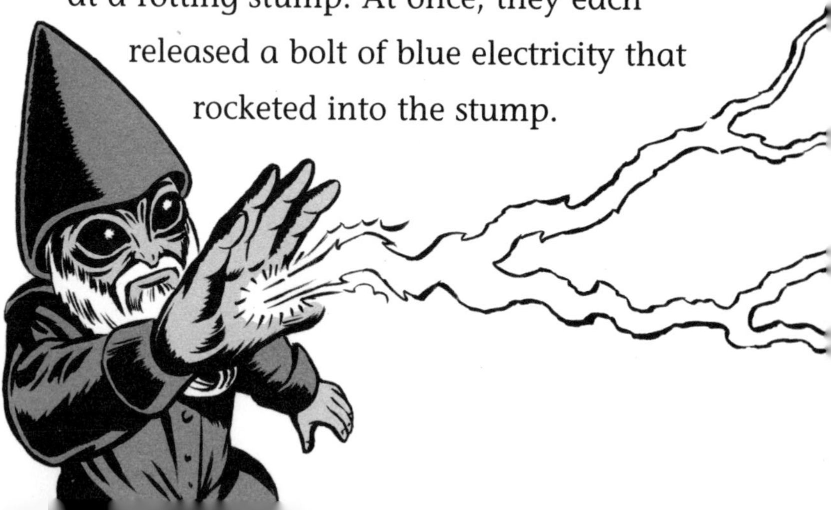

The stump caught on fire. Almost as fast, a jet of water shot up from inside the stump.

The water put out the flames before they could spread.

"We do not have big machines," Barumph said, "but now we do have something more powerful."

He paused, looking at Mary. Then he added, "Because you have been a friend to us, we are giving you fair warning. You have one day to stop your kind from invading our forest ever again. If you cannot stop them, we will burn down more than your friend's barn."

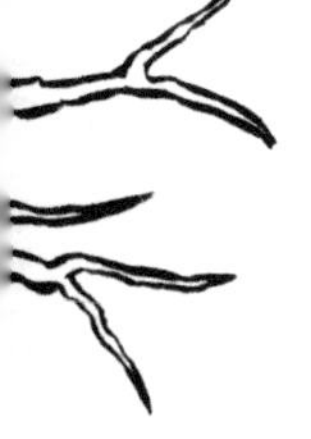

Chapter 6

SOMETHING BIG

Mary's heart began to race. She tried to calm down, but couldn't. She opened her mouth, but no words came out. Then she turned and ran.

Isabel was riding Red Delicious when Mary arrived at the farm. She stopped her horse when she saw Mary. "What are you doing here?" Isabel asked, smiling.

"I have something big to tell you," Mary said. She looked around.

Isabel's dad and Kyle were clearing out what was left of the barn. "But not here," Mary said, more quietly. "Somewhere we won't be interrupted. And we have to be quick."

In the field between the farm and the forest, Mary told Isabel about the gnomes and what they asked of her.

"You said it was something big," Isabel said. "These people sound pretty tiny to me."

"We don't have time for jokes," Mary said.

"Why haven't I ever seen any of them?" Isabel asked.

"I only see them when I'm alone, and only because . . ." Mary stopped.

"Because of what happened to you in the forest that time, right?" Isabel asked.

Mary nodded. "Now I have to tell my dad," she said. "That means that I have to tell him what I just told you . . . and more. And I have to tell you, too."

Isabel shook her head. "You don't have to tell me," she said. "If you want to keep it to yourself, it's okay."

"No, I've kept enough to myself," Mary said. "The only way I'm going to stop Barumph is by telling the truth."

"The gnomes aren't going to like that," Isabel said.

"They didn't tell me I had to continue hiding their existence," Mary said. "The only way I'll get my dad to do this is by telling the truth."

Isabel leaned forward. "Well, if you want to tell me, you can," she said. "I'm all ears."

Mary took a deep breath. "Okay," she began. "It happened when I was six. It was summer vacation, and I went to work with my dad one day because my mom couldn't find a babysitter for me. Dad was working in the forest because his company was planning to cut down a bunch of trees to build condos. While he was busy talking to his people, I wandered off."

"You still do that," Isabel said.

"I don't remember how long I walked," Mary went on, "but it must've been a while because the gnomes live really deep in the woods. Somewhere near there, I fell through a hole into an underground cave."

She paused, then went on, "I was down really deep. There was no way I could climb out. I called for help, but no one came."

"Please tell me your dad heard you!" Isabel said.

"The story has a happy ending," Mary said. "I lived, of course."

"Oh. Right," Isabel said.

Mary smiled. Then she went on, "My dad didn't hear me. But the gnomes did. They dropped a branch through the hole. One of them called down to me. He told me to grab hold of the branch. Then, while I waited, a female gnome stayed near the hole."

Mary smiled, remembering. She went on, "She talked to me and helped keep me calm, even though I couldn't see her. She told me to take slow, deep breaths. I found out later her name was Fetty. She was Jillbell's mother."

"So she's the wife of the bad gnome, Barumph, right?" Isabel asked.

"Barumph isn't bad," Mary said. "He's just scared."

"He burned down my barn," Isabel said. "Maybe he's scared, but he's still bad."

"Fetty wasn't bad," Mary told her. "She really helped me when I was down there. When I was nine, I found out that she had been killed. By a bulldozer."

"That's terrible," Isabel said. "But how did they get you out of the cave?"

"Simple," Mary said. "They flooded it."

"What?" Isabel asked.

"The gnomes have a network of underground tunnels," Mary explained. "Some of their tunnels are hollow. They use the hollow tunnels as roads. Some of the tunnels are sealed off at both ends and filled with water. The gnomes control it all. They use it to drink, wash clothes, take baths, whatever. And when they need to, they can release a lot of it at once."

"Wow. If you'd told me this earlier, I would never have complained about going to the forest all the time," Isabel said. "It's so cool!"

"It is cool," Mary said, smiling. "So when I was in the cave, they gave me a warning. Then water started rushing in."

She took a deep breath. Then she said, "The branch they'd thrown down helped me stay afloat and keep my head above the water. I held onto that branch so tight! In a few minutes, the water filled pretty much the whole cave, lifting me up to the top. I reached out of the hole and pulled myself out."

"Then what?" Isabel asked. "I'm guessing you couldn't give them a hug."

Mary said, "No, but I thanked them over and over. They were nice, but I could tell they were scared. I heard my dad and his crew calling for me. We didn't have much time to talk, but the gnomes and I made a deal."

"What was it?" Isabel asked. "What did you promise them?"

"They said I could come back and visit them if I promised never to tell anyone else about them," Mary said. "When I got older, the deal changed. They started asking me to stop my father and other developers from cutting down their forest."

"How'd they expect you to do that?" Isabel asked.

"Well, since my dad almost lost me in those woods, his company figured it would be hard for him to work there," Mary explained. "There were plenty of other sites to build on, so they canceled the condo project. For a few years, anyway."

Isabel glanced over at the trees. "I never would've guessed that you were obsessed with the forest because of gnomes," she said.

"Now you know," Mary said. "And now I've got to talk to my dad. Barumph said I could only have one day."

"I'll come with you," Isabel said. "And I'm sorry about giving you a hard time for going to the forest. I was being a moron, not a best friend."

"It's okay," Mary said, smiling. "Now let's go to my house. We have to save the forest."

Chapter 7

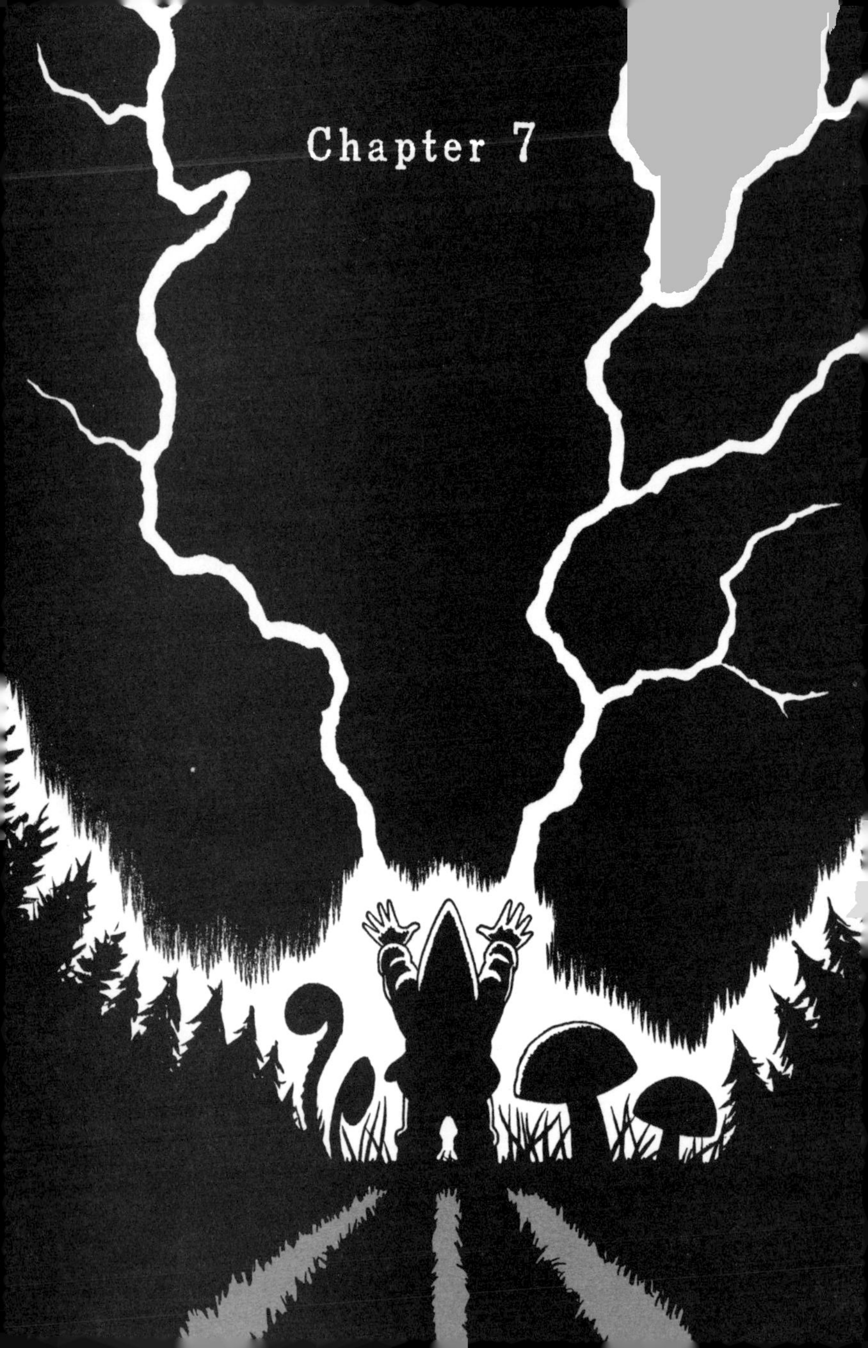

HELP EACH OTHER

Mary told her parents everything. "I know it's hard to believe," she said when she'd finished. "But think back to the day I got lost. You found me soaking wet with no water in sight."

"I do believe you," her dad said. "But this is much bigger than the woods," he added. "This is international news."

"You can't tell anyone," Mary said. "I promised, and I owe them. They saved my life."

"Mary, honey, I know," Dad said. "But a discovery like this is historic. The world needs to know."

"But Mr. Petit," Isabel said, "they will do bad things if we don't do what they say."

"I'm really not worried about a bunch of four-inch-tall people," Mary's dad said.

"They can sneak almost anywhere without being seen," Isabel said. "Even the Army can't do that."

"Stop!" Mary said. "I found them, I made the deal with them, and we're not telling anyone about them!"

She took a deep breath. Then she went on, "Dad, it's almost dark. We have less than half a day. Can you stop people from cutting down any more of the forest or not?"

Her father sighed. "This is not a small favor you're asking," he said. "We're talking about a lot of people's jobs."

"No, I'm talking about our lives," Mary said. "You're not taking the gnomes seriously."

"Yes, I am," her dad said. "But I can't give an instant answer. I know it seems like we're running out of time, but believe me, I've had to make big decisions before. I believe you, and now I'm asking you to trust me."

* * *

Later that evening, Mary and Isabel sat together on Mary's porch. Suddenly, Isabel saw something dart across the steps. Then Jillbell was standing on Mary's knee. Isabel almost screamed.

"Jillbell!" Mary said. "What are you doing here? How'd you find me?"

"I have visited you many times, ever since my mama died," Jillbell admitted. "I just never had the courage to show myself. My mama often told my papa that humans cannot be as bad as we thought if there are more like you. But she would not have liked it if she knew I was coming here."

Isabel was still staring. "Jillbell, this is my friend Isabel," Mary said.

"Pleased to meet you," Jillbell said. Isabel kept staring.

"Don't mind her," Mary said. "She's never seen a gnome before."

"I am sure you can guess why I am here," Jillbell said. "What did your papa decide?"

"He's still thinking about it," Mary said sadly. "What about your dad?"

"I am scared," Jillbell admitted. "I think he may do something tonight."

"That's not fair!" Mary said. "He gave me until tomorrow!"

"It's because of my mama," Jillbell said. "He misses her so much. He feels he already waited too long. Now with this new lightning power —" She stopped and shook her head.

"Do you have it too?" Mary asked.

"No. Only a few of us do," Jillbell said. "But that's enough of us to do a lot of damage."

"Jillbell, we have to help each other," Mary said quietly.

In the distance, a white streak ripped across the sky. It looked like lightning, except that it traveled up, not down.

"That came from the forest," Mary said.

"Oh no," Jillbell said. "It's too late."

"Not yet. We have to get there as fast as we can," Mary said.

"I know just the way," said Isabel.

Chapter 8

PROTECTED HABITAT

Red Delicious galloped through the field next to the forest.

Mary and Isabel were on his back. Jillbell was tucked into one of Mary's pockets.

They reached the forest. Isabel guided Red Delicious through the trees. Every time a bolt of lightning flashed, the horse tried to turn around, but Isabel kept patting and reassuring him.

As they neared the gnome village, a spear of lightning shot at them from the little clearing.

"My papa does not know that I am with you," Jillbell said nervously.

The horse stopped. "Red Delicious is scared to go any closer," Isabel said. "Smart horse."

The girls got off the horse and tied his reins to a tree. Another lightning spear whizzed past them.

Mary stood in front of Isabel and took a deep breath. "Barumph!" she called. "Please stop! It's Mary! You said I could have a day to change their minds!"

"We have Jillbell!" Isabel added.

The lightning stopped.

"She's not hurt," Mary said quickly. "She's my friend!"

The girls walked toward the clearing. Fifty or more gnomes stood there. Mary could see that some of their hands were glowing.

"I have good news," Mary said. "My father says we will protect the forest."

"He didn't say that," Isabel whispered.

"Shh!" Mary said. "I have a plan."

"Did you tell him about us?" Barumph asked.

"I had to," Mary admitted. "But there is a solution that will save your forest. The only way to keep out other builders is to say that the forest is home to an endangered species."

"We are not an endangered species!" Barumph said angrily.

"No," Mary said. "There is another endangered species here. We'll tell everyone that the forest is a protected habitat for the Karner blue butterfly. Then you will be protected too."

Barumph asked, "How can we trust you?"

Jillbell scrambled down Mary's leg and ran to her father. He hugged her. "Mama would tell us to trust them," Jillbell told him.

"Your people and mine are not all that different," Mary told Barumph. "Neither listens to their daughters all the time, but both love their daughters. And you're builders, too. Your tunnels prove that."

"We are nothing like your kind!" Sleb yelled, stepping into view. "Butterflies won't save us! This ends now!" With both hands, he fired lightning at the tree closest to Mary and Isabel.

The tree exploded into flames. The fire spread to several other trees.

In seconds, the forest glowed orange and deadly.

Chapter 9

SMALL HANDS

Most of the gnomes ran underground. Red Delicious stomped the ground and whinnied loudly. Mary and Isabel clung to each other. The fire was destroying all the brush around them.

"Jillbell! Jillbell!" Mary called. She felt a poke on her shoe and looked down to see the little gnome. "The water tunnels!" Mary said. "We have to open as many as we can! Can you do it?"

Jillbell nodded. Then she disappeared.

Mary and Isabel tried to get back to Red Delicious, but flames blocked their way.

The ground began to shake slightly. A second later, water shot up from a hole in the ground, but it only put out a small part of the fire.

"It's not enough," Mary cried.

A heavy tree branch, wrapped in flames, crashed in front of them

"We're going to die!" screamed Isabel.

"Jillbell! Help us!" Mary yelled. "Hurry!"

The ground shook again. This time the tremor was more powerful. Then dozens of geysers erupted. The water drenched the entire area. Soon, the fire was out.

The girls waited for several minutes. None of the gnomes returned.

Back at Isabel's house, Mary called her parents. They arrived in a few minutes.

The girls told the adults what happened. "We'll have to call the papers about the butterflies," Mary's father said. "I've been wanting to do that for a long time, but I knew it might make my company mad if they couldn't work in the forest. Now I have no excuse to not tell everyone about the endangered butterflies."

"You didn't make that up?" Isabel asked Mary.

"My dad told me about the blue butterflies years ago," Mary said. "I learned they were endangered back in sixth grade when I was doing a report. I wish I would've thought of it sooner. Maybe some of the gnomes wouldn't have died. Like Jillbell's mother."

That night, Mary slept over at Isabel's farm. In the morning, when the girls looked outside, they saw a brand-new barn. It had been built overnight by very small hands using very small tools.

About the Author

Marc Tyler Nobleman has written books on everything from ghosts to Groundhog Day, belly flops to the Battle of the Little Bighorn, Superman to summertime activities. Besides writing books, he is also a cartoonist whose work has appeared in more than 100 magazines.

About the Illustrator

Bradford Kendall has enjoyed drawing for as long as he can remember. As a boy, he loved to read comic books and watch old monster movies. He graduated from the Rhode Island School of Design with a BFA in Illustration. Bradford lives in Providence, Rhode Island with his wife, Leigh, and their two children, Lily and Stephen. They also have a cat named Hansel and a dog named Gretel.

Glossary

bolts (BOHLTS)—flashes of lightning

charred (CHARD)—burnt

cycle (SYE-kuhl)—a series of events repeated over and over again

endangered species (en-DAYN-jurd SPEE-seez)—a type of plant or animal that is in danger of becoming extinct

gnomes (NOHMZ)—small people who live in the woods, according to legend

habitat (HAB-uh-tat)—the place in which an animal or plant lives

historic (hiss-TOR-ik)—something that will be seen as important in the future

hollow (HOL-oh)—if something is hollow, it has an empty space inside it

obsessed (uhb-SESSD)—if you're obsessed with something, you think about it all the time

remains (ri-MAINZ)—things left over

Discussion Questions

1. Do you believe in gnomes? Why or why not?

2. Mary says that fathers don't always listen to their daughters. What do you think?

3. If a friend told you that he or she knew gnomes, what would you think? Would you believe your friend? Why or why not?

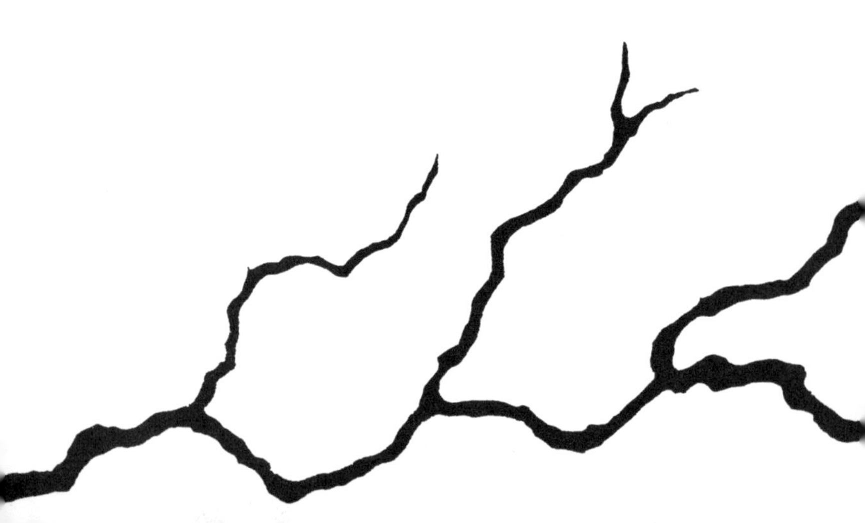

Writing Prompts

1. Write a newspaper article that tells the world about the gnomes found in the forest.

2. What do you think happens after this book ends? Write a chapter that picks up where this book leaves off.

3. Pretend you're Jillbell. Write a letter to Mary describing a normal day in the gnome village.